CW01085969

Don't stop dreaming

A book for children, boys and girls to help them increase motivation, self-esteem, courage, inner strength, respect, dreams, self-confidence

SERENA R. MANCINI

Copyright © 2021 Serena R. Mancini

All rights reserved

ISBN: 9798358700703

INDICE

INTRODUCTION

Combined in many magical stories, words have the power to free ourselves from fear, conformity, and prejudice. Serena R. Mancini's brilliant pen brings to life **five incredible characters**: little boys and girls who face the complexity of life with friends, teachers, and parents. There's Lara, a little girl who decides to become a scientist and sets out to discover the truth with capital V, only to discover that beauty is all about the uniqueness of the people you meet along the way. And then, three schoolmates decide to help each other achieve their **dreams**. Each story comes with a **colouring page** and an **supplementary section** where the writer shares the "behind the scenes" of each piece along with personal anecdotes and **childhood memories**.

The words that can never be missed? Hope, **courage**, cooperation, selflessness, **participation**, loyalty, self-esteem and **motivation**. These are complex topics that we as educators sometimes undervalue, but are the foundations of **tomorrow's adults**.

In detail:

• A story about **bullying** and **cyberbullying** with a supplementary section containing practical tips to help kids solve communication problems with their peers, both online and offline.

• A story about overcoming the **fear of failure**. We learn by our mistakes, especially when we meet people who know how to recognise kid's talents!

• What can we learn from **Nature**? In a Natural History Museum, a child finds out that many technological inventions wouldn't exist without the help of flowers, birds, plants, mammals, and insects!

• **Sharing and altruism** are the engines of society. You can double the fun by joining together the small games of many kids!

• *Much more!*

Serena R. Mancini's precious work takes young readers by the hand and helps them learn about themselves and the world around them. Parents and teachers can then discuss and deepen the **moral of her stories** so that children can get answers to all their questions.

Indeed, the Whys of children are always synonymous with great and wonderful discoveries!

Happy reading!

Serena R. Mancini

What's the origin of these stories?

What's the secret to unleashing the imagination, flying on the wings of inspiration, and finding the best idea?

My little reader, I thought a lot before writing the book you're holding in your hands. Initially, I traveled around the world exploring mysterious neighbourhoods. You know, I felt like a tourist who'd just landed on another planet, like Jupiter or Saturn. After unpacking, I chatted with my neighbours. Each spoke a different language - some filled with 's', others full of 'r' and 'k'. Finally, while eating chocolate ice cream under a hot summer sun and sipping steaming hot chocolate on a cold winter night, I started writing non-stop in my notebook.

What's that? – you may be wondering. A notebook is a workbook, a personal diary, and a writer's best friend.

Day after day, word after word, I gained a new perspective on the world through my travels.

I danced to songs sung in Spanish or Russian, ate traditional dishes very different from pizza and pasta with tomato sauce, and had a thousand adventures to write brand new stories.

Just like the striker who wants to score the winning goal, I raced around the earth, dribbling boredom and habits. Meanwhile, I collected enough food for thought to write many, many exciting stories. In my free time I read fantasy and romantic books, I immersed myself in the mysteries of a thriller and held my breath for the plot twists of an adventure novel.

At this point, you may ask yourself: "and you? Did you write your stories?".

Yes Sir, these are the first stories I've written and published. The protagonists are all brave and intelligent kids, just like you. A little girl never stops asking her parents "why" and discovers that we all see the world differently; three friends achieve their dreams with music, dribbles, and... stars! A little nature lover open his heart to the plants, fossils, and insects he discovers in London's parks and museums to invent many innovative solutions. Maybe he'll become a scientist with a long beard, longer than the Nile! If you keep reading, you'll also meet a... *record teacher*! I've never heard anyone do anything so cunning and ingenious to keep bullies under control.

And I've seen all these incredible characters with my own eyes. I swear.

Pinky promise!

My little reader, the trips I've taken around the world have worn me out, you know? Now I, too, have a long beard like that of a scientist and my legs hurt from long walks in the desert, in the woods or by the sea. So, I sat down at my desk, lit a white candle, took a sharpener and honed my trusty pencil. It's time to turn my notebook full of ideas into **five stories with capital "S" that you can read on your own, or perhaps with your mom and dad**.

When? In the morning or before you go to sleep at night. If you love waking up with the light of dawn like me, you can soak a cookie in hot milk while learning the importance of cooperation, altruism, respect for Nature, the value of diversity and the importance of having not one, but a thousand dreams in the drawer. ***Think big!***

If you'd rather glide over Neverland when the Moon's high in the sky and you're too tired to hold back the yawns, ask your parents to tuck you in as you hold my little book in your little hands.

Curious to know more? Then I'd like to personally welcome

you to the "city of paper" that I have built... ops, written for you to make you independent, help you grow and understand the world. Because travels and adventures may be "grown-up things", but **fantasy is a treasure kept in every kid's heart and mind, so take care of it and NEVER abandon it!**

Imagination is faster than cars, buses, trams, cruise ships and airplanes flying above the clouds. And you know what? It is even more comfortable! Lie down on your little bed or sit in your favourite armchair, open your eyes and follow me in this one-of-a-kind editorial experiment. Trust me when I say that every day will be an unforgettable and extraordinary adventure! To put it in the words of my "colleague" Gianni Rodari, someone who knew a lot about stories: "I believe that fairy tales, old and new, can help educate the mind. The fairy tale is the place for all hypotheses: it lets us enter reality through new paths, it helps kids learn about the world".

WHY? WHY? WHY?

A story to learn about the world

From behind an oak, Lara admires the colours of autumn. Light wind swirls lift the red, yellow, and brown leaves, causing them to fall back onto pinecones and thin pine needles. She really likes the smell of the resin. For this reason, she got into the habit of walking in her neighbourhood's park after school. The park is full of children playing - bundled in coloured scarves, gloves and hats with wool pom-poms - and parents chatting on wooden benches, throwing balls or pushing swings. She feels like a grown-up: she can play in the playground even when mum and dad are busy at work. Her dear Grandma Camilla lives "two minutes from the park" - as her mother says. "She always keeps an eye on you!" she concludes.

Lara is happy. It's like she's an adventurer, free to explore every corner of the park, making new friends, and eating the ham sandwich her dad made that morning. It's a beautiful day and her sneakers produce a slight "crick crack" when in contact with the dry leaves under her feet.

Suddenly, Lara looks up: "**Why** have the trees changed colour?" - she wonders. Pines and oaks have red and yellow foliage. There's no sign of spring emerald green anymore. As she eats her delicious sandwich in small bites, she grabs her school diary and her favourite pen from her backpack.

She's made up her mind! When she grows up, she will become a scientist and will discover all the secrets of Nature. So why not start now?

"Who knows who's going to give me the right answer?", she wonders with the same serious and absorbed face as her math teacher.

After walking for a while, she comes across a kiosk that sells sandwiches, ice cream, and cold drinks. The man at the cashier immediately catches her attention: he has a long black moustache, very thick sideburns and red cheeks from the cold. Clouds of steam come out of his smiling mouth. Briskly, Lara approaches him.

«Excuse me, sir!", she shouts, standing on tiptoe to get noticed by the funny salesman.

"Hello kid, how can I help you?", he replies kindly"

"I have a question for you ... Can you tell me why the leaves on the trees changed colour in autumn?" she asks, clutching the coloured pen and the diary where she takes notes. The little man frowns and looks up at the branches of the trees.

"*Mumble, mumble*! That's a good question!", he says. "The leaves turn yellow and red because the wind blows the green colour away!"

Lara writes down the answer of her new friend in the

"Science Notebook" and continues walking ... but not before buying a handful of orange candies! Nearby, she runs into an elderly lady. She's sitting on a bench with her legs crossed. Her red enamelled fingers are holding a colourful magazine.

"Madam, can I ask you a question?", Lara asks in a shrill voice, louder than she wants it to be. She can't contain her excitement! The elderly woman jumps, looking left and right. She must have been immersed in some super-secret gossip!

"Of course, darling! I'm all ears ... You are not lost, are you?", she asks alarmed.

"No, no, my grandma lives nearby. I just want to know why the leaves on the trees have changed colour!

"Oh, that's easy!" says the lady, putting her hand on her chest to fix the crimson scarf. "They changed colours to make the lawn orange and red... otherwise it would have stayed just green! Don't you see how beautiful it is now? "

"Yes, it is fantastic!" Lara answers.

That evening at home, Lara approaches her mom, who's chopping juicy tomatoes to prepare a delicious sauce for dipping fresh bread bought from a baker and baked the "old" way, in a wood oven.

"Mom, can I ask you a question?"

"Tell me Lara!" she replies. In the meantime, she puts the pot on the stove and the oil starts sizzling.

"Why did the leaves on the trees changed colour?" Lara asks, clutching her beloved diary.

"Ah, you went to the park today! Well, the leaves change colour because the cold of autumn dries up the highest branches of the trees!"

Little Lara walks quickly back to her room. She's very confused. Why did the adults give her different answers? Are autumn trees red and yellow because the wind blows away the green colour? Is it because the lawn looks prettier this way? Or could it be that the cold dries out the highest branches?

What a headache! Who lied among them?

"What a mystery!" Lara whispers to herself.

So, the next day, she decides to ask another question. She starts questioning Miss Mia, her favourite teacher, who always has an intelligent answer to all doubts in the class. Lara's heart pounds in her chest.

«Miss Mia, why is studying so important?».

Pleasantly surprised by the question, Miss Mia replies: "because when you grow up you will be a good, responsible woman, you will speak many foreign languages, and you will know how to reckon and recite poetry. That's the only way you can live the life of your dreams!"

A few hours later, Lara asks the same question to her dear Grandma Camilla.

"Grandma, grandma why is studying so important?"

Grandma Camilla looks at her with a contented look while stroking the head of her red cat, a five-year-old Siamese named Cleo. The old lady turns off the tv's hum and watches Lara with her teal eyes, behind thick eyeglasses.

"My little Lara, studying allows you to travel with your imagination and discover many new things," she tells her.

Finally, Lara turns to her dad. He's a very tall man, always wearing a well-ironed shirt that smells like laundry. He works for an insurance company, although Lara doesn't know exactly what that means.

"Dad, why is studying so important?", she asks for the third time.

"Simple," he replies. "When you grow up, you'll find a good job that makes you happy." He continues to eat a delicious piece of cake from the town's most famous pastry shop without looking up.

Lara feels even more confused than the day before. How come everyone has a different answer to her thousand whys? Who's right? Her very intelligent teacher, her dear Grandma Camilla, or her greedy dad?

How can I find out the truth?

Lara decides to keep asking a thousand questions, and she notes the answers of her new friends in the "Science Notebook". After a few weeks, she fills the blank pages with ideas, questions, curiosities and ... little scribbles of boredom! The day of her birthday finally arrives. Lara turns eight and her parents decide to surprise her. They plan a weekend in the mountains with her best friends: Zoe, Andrea, and Benny.

The birthday girl wakes up early. She is too excited to stay warm under the covers. She wants to open her parents' gifts and pack her backpack. It is a red and blue floral backpack that Uncle Micky gave her for Christmas three years ago.

She's kept it with great care. Like her dad, Lara loves to hold onto things, especially if they're a bit worn out. Mum, on the other hand, doesn't think the same way: if she could, she'd throw everything she deems "unnecessary" away - that's what she says. Lara packs her camera, a canary yellow scarf, and a spare pair of long wool socks. And, of course, her ever-present diary of questions.

"Will there be snow, dad?" she asks an hour later, as he jumps with joy on the doorstep. Everything's ready for departure.

"I think so, sweetheart! Let's go see," he replies, gently disheveling her blonde tuft.

It's true that happiness takes very little! The mountain air is cold, but the view is wonderful. As dad's flaming red four-wheeler rides along snowy climbs, descents, and hairpin bends, Lara keeps her nose glued to the window. Her friend Betty keeps sighing "Wow!" and «Oh!», while Andrea is engaged in an intense conversation with Lara's dad about the types of engines used in Formula 1. A true racing fan, him!

Finally, the car stops near a cracked space. The pines are tall and straight like the city's street lamps, and the scent of Nature fills Lara's nostrils with its intoxicating sweetness.

"It's the best day of my life!" She thinks. However, a sudden thought crosses her mind. <u>She hasn't figured out yet why all adults answer her questions differently</u>. Is it possible no one can solve this mystery? Lara looks around: Andrea won't be able to help her - he's too obsessed with video games and cars to support her "Search for the Truth" - while Zoe and Benny have promised not to tell anyone about her strange obsession with questions. However, they told her outright "we think you shouldn't trust adults. My father often says that some "grown-ups" never really grow up," concluded Benny months earlier.

The day flies by. Zoe stumbles on a large snowy branch and ends up upside down in the snow, under everyone's amused gaze; mom drops her cheese sandwich.

"Because my fingers are frozen" - she justifies herself, blushing from embarrassment and disappointment - while dad starts picking out a long list of rock songs for the return trip, without realizing no one likes long choruses with electric guitar and loud drums. Finally, at the thick of it, something special happens.

Very special indeed!

Lara and her family run into a park ranger. The man wears a funny feathered cap and a military uniform - just like the shooter characters of Andrea's favourite video games - and has dark, lively eyes that settle on the cold face of the birthday girl.

"Happy birthday!" - he wishes her, making her blush. «I take care of the park and its inhabitants: birds, insects, little spiders, but also deers, wild boars and chamois. There are tons of animals to discover in the mountains. What a great idea your dad had taking you here, the view is amazing Let's go, I'll guide you to the highest point!" he said, venturing into the snowy grass in his rubber boots. Lara can't wait and follows the Ranger with her heart in her throat. After a few minutes of walking - which seems like hours to Lara - the group reaches the top of a hill surrounded by wind, trees and... a wonderful sunset! The aspiring little scientist is very tired: she's been walking all day and she's so hungry she scares Zoe with the "Grrr!" Of her grouchy stomach. The roar of a lion! However, she can't resist taking a souvenir photo with the Ranger. Behind her - who's all smiling and blushing with emotion - an unforgettable scenario opens up: the sky's fiery sunset hues are reflected in the white snow that covers the trees. To her right, a mirror of water in the distance reminds her of the fake pond she used to prepare for the Nativity under Grandma Camilla's watchful eye. To her left, the mountain looms in all its rocky might. Oh, how tall and scary it is up close! Lara keeps taking pictures, never stopping, until the Ranger approaches to ask: "you're getting old, huh? Do you already know what job you want to do when you grow up?". «Of course, I will be a scientist and I will unravel all the mysteries of Nature. "I want to know why everything happens ... Look!" she suddenly says, opening her beloved backpack with a decisive gesture. She hands her friend the "Science Notebook" where she recorded the results of her research, carefully protecting it from the humidity of the snow. "Maybe we'll be colleagues someday"

- says Lara, illustrating in detail the result of weeks of questions. Then, an idea crosses her mind: maybe the park ranger knows why adults answer her questions differently.

"C-can I ask you a question?" she asks.

"Sure, that's why I'm here!" the Ranger answers, leaning against a pine trunk.

"Why do you grownups all answer differently?" It's impossible to become a good scientist if you never agree on anything. "Could someone be lying to me?" - Lara asks, frowning, **arms crossed** over **chest.** She is very angry with the adults and their oddness!

With a bright smile, the Ranger moves closer.

"What do you see in front of you?" he asks.

"Er... a lake to the right and a mountain to the left. But what does this have to do with it? " asks Lara, who's even more confused now!

«Well done, Lara! Now cover your left eye with your hand and tell me what you see! "

As she follows the Ranger's invitation, her lower lip is bitten with a bit of doubt. And indeed ... "I only see the lake now," she says.

"What if I now ask you to open the left eye and cover the right?"

«I only see the mountain...» Lara replies, as her new friend's reasoning finally starts making sense to her.

"And now tell me ... which of the three answers you gave me is a lie?" asks the Ranger.

"Well, none ... Indeed, it makes sense!" she replies, opening her eyes wide, surprised.

How come she didn't think of it before?

"All the answers in your notebook are true. You know, we're all special, we live and face once-in-a-lifetime adventures. In addition, everyone has a memory drawer filled with unique memories. It's right here ... " the Ranger explains, tapping his index finger on his head. "Every person you meet along the way is like a forest to explore. After hikes and descents, sightings, picnics, and long walks, you'll figure out why someone gave you that particular answer. But don't think your mom, granny, friends or strangers in the park are lying to you. The world is wonderful because... we all have so many worlds inside us!"

"S-So, should I stop asking questions?" Lara asks, bending her

head to one side.

"Not at all! Keep asking questions, my very intelligent scientist, because that's the only way you'll be able to truly understand the world around you!"

As she admires snowy meadows and sky-high clouds inflamed by the sunset's colours, she feels euphoric. She can't wait to discover the secrets of the world thanks to her thousand "whys".

This is just the beginning!

The author says…

A few years ago, José Saramago, a much better and more experienced writer than me, said: "Old age starts when curiosity disappears." I wrote this sentence in my notebook of creative ideas and let it mature month after month - a bit like a caterpillar becoming a butterfly! Finally, during my wacky travels around the world, I met a little girl named Lara.

She was sitting on the train with her mum and dad, and she never stopped pointing out the view from the window, the heavy suitcases of the other passengers, the red ticket, the conductor's uniform and the nice hostesses who delivered lunch, asking the "Whys" of everything around her. As I was tired and bored from the long journey, my mind instantly went to the quote by Mr. Samarago.
«Here's an idea for a new story!» - I said to myself adjusting the hat over my head. Yes, this is my little twitch of narrative inspiration! Whenever I feel a good story coming, I wear my

cap, I take my notebook, open it to a blank page, and start writing the first draft.

Why?

Because **asking questions is wonderful**. Questions make us human, smart, funny, creative and very, very wise! But in the end, we just get used to the reality around us. We recognise the sound of the rain and the traffic, the taste of a chocolate ice cream and the barking of a dog. Past experiences affect our perception of the world. In the same way we learn to solve second degree equations at school after learning first degree equations, or study Ancient Greece before the Middle Ages and the Renaissance, life teaches us lessons that make us more and more knowledgeable over time. Curiosity gets replaced by habit.

It's for this reason that childhood is such a special time: kids have empty minds to fill with drawings, scribbles, phrases, letters, and words to invent! And as we grow up, we can all "remain children".

How?

Keeping in mind that life's thousand whys deserve more

than one answer!

Question after question, we'll learn something new, we'll keep our fears under control, we'll meet people who think differently, and we'll stop being afraid of failing. Just like Lara, the little girl I accidentally met on a train to Berlin, you and your parents can cultivate your curiosity. *To grow together.*

A TRIP TO THE MUSEUM OF NATURAL HISTORY

The incredible adventures of a child who solves problems with the help of Mother Nature

"English essay: a day at the Natural History Museum in London.

Dear teacher, my name is Tim, and I'm 8 years old. When I grow up, I want to ~~faind~~ find dinosaur fossils and learn all about T-Rex and pterodactyls. Meanwhile, I'll tell you about my trip to the Natural History Museum in London. Do you know how much I ~~laiked~~ liked it?".

It's been 25 years since I, Timothy McCarthy, first stepped foot in a museum. This morning - a sunny spring morning with birds chirping excitedly and my neighbours watering the lawn while listening to the 91.5 radio station - I accidentally found an old memory box in the cellar. Since I'm allergic to dust, I started sneezing and coughing as hard as I could, while my nose turned red like a clown's and my eyes swelled up like those of a toad.

«Craaa!»

In the mysterious trunk of my past, I found old childhood photographs - and I must say I look a lot like my dad now! - but also marbles, yellowed plushes, a pair of smelly socks worn in who knows what football match and even a thin gold-edged folder containing some old school memorabilia: my English essays, some math tests and a class photo dating back a long, long time ago. That's how I found my first essay about the trip I took to the Natural History Museum.

I remember that day like it was yesterday.

Right there, in the quiet, somewhat cold corridors of the insect collection, I decided to devote my life to studying Nature in all its forms.

But let's do this in an order, my little reader.

When I was eight, I used to think museums were dusty, super-boring places to spend a rainy afternoon (in the absence of video games). So, I woke up in a bad mood. In the kitchen, my mom welcomed me with her usual bright smile and open arms: «How beautiful! Your first trip to London! Aren't you happy, Tim? "

"Mmmh" - I mumbled in response, pouring more milk on my chocolate cereal. Twenty-five years later, my breakfast habits haven't changed. *I'm a big fan of chocolate cereal!*

"Well, why the long face?" - she asked me.

"I don't want to go to the Museum, and then you said I'm allOrgic to dust!"

"It's allergic, Tim, and you won't find a speck of dust at the Natural History Museum. And then, who's a fan of dinosaurs and other ... scary creatures!" my mother exclaimed, tickling me. Trying to hold back the laughter so as not to spill my cereal on the table, I put on my sneakers and ran to the nearest bus stop.

Direction?

South Kensington, Exhibition Road. I would've made it to the museum on time. Speaking of the Museum. Imagine my surprise when I got off the bus with my sleepy eyes. I looked up and ... "Wow!" - I shouted. In front of me stood a huge facade decorated with floral themes, not the old and boring museum I had imagined. The two towers on either side of the central staircase silently invited me in. Around me, researchers in shirts and eyeglasses walked briskly with black leather folders in their right hands. Dinosaur Researchers! - I thought. The bad mood I had this morning disappeared like the birthday cake Dad had baked for me a week earlier. I was happy, excited and... electrified like a light bulb! I waited for my friends and Miss Paula so I could see the beautiful rooms of the Museum:

over 70 million exhibits - that's a lot of zeros, believe me - grouped into five main collections: entomology, mineralogy, palaeontology, zoology, and botany.

These mysterious words swirled in my head confusingly back then: everything was new, fascinating, and mysterious. I started to believe that the Natural History Museum was a magical place because after a few minutes I felt... at home! I'd never experienced such emotion, not even on the football field where my best friend Fred and I trained twice a week. We met our guide, a lady in her forties with her hair elegantly styled in a bun.

My classmate Mary giggled enviously: "She looks like a ballet dancer, not a scientist!" she started gossiping. Instead of listening to her, I turned away. Taking my notebook out of my pocket, I got as close as I could to Miss Vera. The morning passed quickly between chemistry experiments and souvenir pictures. Finally, after a quick sandwich break, we took part in a super-exclusive workshop.

Vera explained something really interesting to us.

'Some brilliant researchers have been observing Nature's manifestations for years. The result? They took inspiration from Mother Earth to recreate the very useful technological objects we use every day!" she said. We all looked around, confused. Seeing our confusion, Miss Vera explained: "Come closer! See this black-winged butterfly in the top case?" A perfectly tuned "yes" came from us in chorus, worthy of a singing contest. The animal was elegant and mysterious. It flapped its wings slowly as it rested on a dewy branch.

"The black butterfly's wings are able to absorb and hold the sunlight. So engineers and scientists tried to recreate the ingenious mechanism of our butterfly friend and made ... *eco-friendly, powerful solar panels*. It's all true!"

I couldn't believe it! Could Nature really make our lives better?

Sensing that the whole class was paying attention, our guide didn't get lost in chatter and continued: "And did you know the shark's a great swimmer? The texture of its skin reduces water resistance. That's why it moves so quickly, suddenly, and dangerously! NASA scientists have made some boats and swimwear for divers with a material inspired by the skin of our shark friends!

Oh, how many fascinating things I discovered that afternoon.

Before leaving the Natural History Museum, I bought "The Big Book of Animals" to study the characteristics of all the species Miss Vera mentioned: insects, spiders, mammals, fish, and so on and so forth! Thrilled, I went home and told my family all the amazing things I learned on my school trip. While talking with my mouth full of mashed potatoes, I gestured like actors do in silent movies - the black-and-white ones my grandparents like so much. My dad wouldn't listen to me and kept changing the channels on the TV while mom hung on my every word.

"I promise we will read the beautiful book you bought together, Tim" - she said, making me the happiest child in the world.

Now, my dear reader, you should know that school was crazy for a few weeks, with lots of tests, multiple choice quizzes, and group exercises. In my spare time, I no longer went to the football field with my best friend Fred, but instead took bus 32 to the library, where I spent time browsing all the picture books in the Zoology section - a word that makes you think of a zoo but has nothing to do with animals locked in cages. In my notebook, I drew spiders, leopards, hummingbirds, and furry bunnies with their characteristics written in the margins: speed, resistance, age, strength, direction, eating habits, and place of origin. Imagination took me on an African safari aboard a Jeep, to the depths of the ocean to look for very rare fish, and high in the sky to watch majestic swooping eagles.

Just closing my eyes was enough to feel a part of the animal kingdom, a piece of the puzzle that makes up the Universe.

And my mom was so proud of my obsession with zoology. We once saw a woman at the supermarket holding her baby to her chest with a blue elastic band. «Mom, mom» - I said, «look! That lady is holding her baby in her arms like koalas and kangaroos do in Australia! They also use a pouch... » - and I started repeating all the information I'd memorised about koalas and kangaroos.

But the real adventure happened a few months later.

It was Sunday morning. The sun was high in the sky, shining

on the grass of our garden. I was still in my pyjamas and night socks eating chocolate cereal and brushing my teeth when...someone yelled out the window!

Didn't that sound like my neighbour, Matt? Matt was a curly redhead with a chubby face full of freckles. Although we weren't great friends, we never fought over toys or bike rides.

So, as I was saying, Matt was screaming his head off. I reached the window and followed my parents outside. We found out Bubble, Matt's cat, had climbed up our tree and was stuck. There it was, with its honey-coloured eyes wide open and a slight look of fear on its face. *Does a cat get vertigo?* I didn't have time to go to the library and investigate!

Before Matt's parents climbed the tree, I shouted: "Wait, wait! We'll make a long long rod that'll reach the kitten!" After a few minutes, we made a rescue tool with strings and scissors and put huge pillows near the tree trunk. Bubble thought our do-it-yourself tool was a fun game and tried to grab it with its paw and... *it lost his balance!*

«Pouf!»

The kitten fell on the soft pillows, meowing and purring on the lap of its lucky owner.

Matt hugged Pouf with teary eyes. "You're a genius, Tim! How did you come up with the idea for the long rod?" - he asked.

"Well, you shouldn't thank me, but rather the giraffes and elephants that inspired me! "They, too, have long necks and sturdy trunks to eat leaves from trees" - I replied, hugging my new friend.

Mom came over and dishevelled my blond tuft with her gentle hands.

"You did a great job, Tim, and I think you'll make a great zoologist!" she said.

It turned out my mom was right.

Over the past 25 years, I've travelled the world looking for species to save, natural habitats to preserve, and wonderful animals to discover. I'll never stop exploring as long as I have the strength to lift my loyal shabby suitcase. I've been to the Amazon and Japan, the cold plains of Russia, and the scorching desert of Morocco.

Though I've been to (almost) every country in the world, I can't help but remember, a little moved, my first school trip to the Natural History Museum in London. Miss Paula. And Miss Vera. The bookseller, Matt and my parents because they believed in me and made me feel like a little man full of talent and ... knowledge!

That's right, knowledge sets us free and helps us improve our lives and the lives of those we love the most!

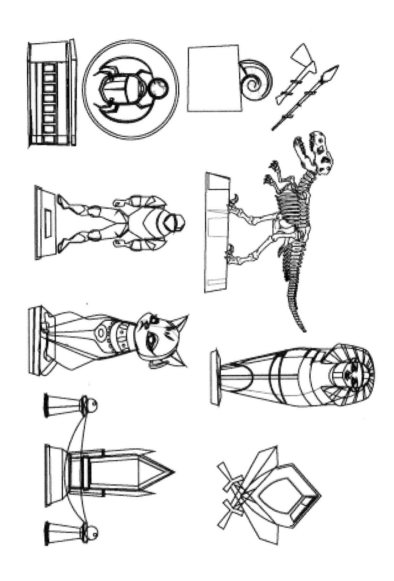

My little reader, the protagonist of this happy ending story looks like me, you know? Like me, he loves nature, museums, and animals. Like him, I can't help but fall asleep with a suitcase ready.

I love travelling and I'm really tireless!

But I'm sure of one curious thing: Timothy, the young zoologist in my story, is a little like you too. Because you, too, have a talent, a hobby, a passion or a dream that you want to fulfil. **Whether you want to be a pop star, a football player, a scientist or a doctor, all it takes is hard work, study and dedication. Always.** Are you ready for the good news? Once you start doing what you love, you won't feel tired or bored. It's the opposite! You'll be 100% committed to achieving your goals.

I, too, was a little scared of judgement before I became a full-time writer.

"What if nobody likes my stories? What if my adventures make everyone yawn?" - I wondered.

In the end, I chose to silence the "little voice of negativity" that kept me from becoming my best self. I put myself out there and sent my first manuscript to a famous Italian publisher.

And do you know what they told me?

"Your book of short stories is great, but we can't publish it right now. We don't think it'll sell that many copies, sorry!"

Ouch, that's a proper refusal!

I kept writing in my notebooks, I read books by better and more famous authors than me, I asked friends, colleagues, and even strangers I met in the cafeteria for their honest opinions, and finally I did it, I made my big dream come true! A small publishing house in my city believed in me and published a nice little book of short stories! Tim, too, achieved a big milestone: after studying animals since he was eight, he became a successful zoologist.

Let's do a little exercise. Don't worry, there are no grades, tests, or surprise questions. This isn't school! Grab a piece of paper and write: "my number 1 wish is ..." or "when I grow up I want to become a ..." and keep it with you at all times, in your secret diary or in your school backpack. When you're feeling down, read the sentence you wrote and think about the little things you can do every day to get closer to your big life goal.

Hold on, Champion!

Bonus sheet – Nature, technology and other mysterious things

Here you are!

Welcome, welcome!

I was looking forward to meeting another young student interested in my zoology lesson at the Natural History Museum in London.

I'm Miss Vera, your guide.

How, how?

Do you want to know what a zoologist does at work? Well, simple! The zoologist is a researcher who studies the behaviour, characteristics and natural habitats of all - absolutely all - animals on the planet. Whenever a new call comes, a scientist emerges from a bush, armed with a camera and a tape recorder, ready to find out all about this mysterious and fascinating species. But that's not the point. If you've read Timothy's story in one breath, you'll know that Nature can be a truly inexhaustible source of inspiration.

In short, photovoltaic panels and tailor-made swimsuits were inspired by the black butterfly and the shark!

But the incredible inventions inspired by nature didn't stop there. During this short workshop, you'll discover <u>3 engineering and technological discoveries that wouldn't have existed without equally incredible plants and animals!</u>

Happy reading!

- Have you ever been on a high-speed train? Japan has "bullet trains" (Shinkansen, 新幹線) that broke the world speed record with a peak speed of 603 kph. Thanks to scientists? Not only that! These fast trains are shaped like the beak of the colourful kingfisher, a small, very fast bird able to catch little fish by launching itself into a nosedive. In the 90s, a Japanese engineer named Eiji Nakatsu, who loved observing animal species in their natural habitats in the Japanese forests, had a stroke of genius. Back in the city, he patented the "nose" of the trains, based on the super-sharp beak of the kingfisher. As they say, the rest is history!

- With their round, yellow eyes, owls are nocturnal

creatures. Their superpower? Their wings are very quiet, so they can glide over their prey totally unnoticed. Researchers at Changchun University in China "copied" owl flight patterns to create low-noise turbines that generate clean, green electricity. The turbines are very similar to those of an airplane, with the only difference that they remain firmly planted on the ground!

- Speaking of high-altitude flights, have you ever seen a professional climber in action? Mountain lovers climb very high rocks using only the strength of their arms and legs. Ugh, what a pain! Once again, Nature comes to our rescue: researchers have analyzed the fingers of geckos - small animals with extraordinary abilities! Nowadays, there are lots of climbing materials on the market inspired by the shape of their legs. They also work on... glass walls!

Not recommended for those suffering from vertigo!

THIS TOY IS MINE!

A story about selflessness for kids who want to change the world.

Together.

Marta's toy box is the most beautiful on the whole beach. She got it from her grandmother - who's Spanish and Marta calls "Abuela" - and it contains bright jewels, beautiful brooches shaped like bees and butterflies, as well as crayons Marta uses under her polka-dot umbrella when the sun's too high for her to play with the ball or swim. From the first day of vacation, Marta's mysterious box caught the attention of all the kids on the beach: some wondered how precious it was, and others wondered how big it was! Some say Marta even pulled out some elegant tea cups made of fine porcelain from her wooden box. Just like those found in any grandmother's or aunt's kitchen!

That's so magical and mysterious!

Could Marta be a little witch? Or could it be that her grandma, *the "Abuela"*, cast a spell on her granddaughter's gift?

In between gossiping and diving in the pool, unlikely hypothesis and vanilla ice cream covered with chocolate chips, one day Marta's little beach neighbours take the initiative and approach her: "Marta, can we play with your magic box?" - they ask.

Marta pouts and turns away.

"No, it's my toy and I decide who can touch it. You can't!" - she shouts, stamping her feet into the hot sand and hiding her mysterious wooden box under her mother's beach towel.

The beach kids are disappointed, but they decide to play

another game together. In the days that follow, they're intrigued by Leo. He wears a hat with a peak and lots of colourful bracelets. He is very tanned and always carries a small bag with some transparent marbles. He's got a dazzling smile and dark eyes like a movie star, which makes the little beach regulars think he's in some TV show! Besides launching his small multicoloured marbles at the speed of light and catching them on the fly, he can also throw them into the air like a circus juggler and catch them behind his back or under his leg. He always wears a Hawaiian shirt - with yellow and purple flowers, his favourite - that flutters in the breeze along with his long, coal-black hair.

In short, whenever there's a slight breeze, Leo looks like a heron about to fly! The kids on the beach admire him a lot, quietly wondering what makes him so strong, good, and charming.

One day, Leo tries in every way to play with his dad. He tries to attract his attention, but the man keeps talking loudly on the cell phone he's holding, without taking his eyes off the hot sand. The little boy pouts, throws his marbles in anger and runs towards the blue coast - under the incredulous gaze of the other children. Some are too shy to talk to him, while others approach the unattended marbles to observe them from up close. They are so beautiful! Sadly, no one has the courage to ask Leo to play with them, so a few minutes after sunset they run back to their parents to close the umbrellas, put on their sandals and go home.

July's long and bright days pass peacefully between lemon slushes and fresh fruit salads. Finally, after all that coming and going of tattooed lifeguards, busy moms, panting dads, and talented volleyball or ping-pong players, a new kid shows up. He wears a colourful hat - like the traditional sombrero of Mexican guitarists - and has the coolest toy anyone's ever seen: a remote-controlled truck that digs tunnels in the sand with... engineering precision! That thing is more useful than a thousand rakes and more powerful than any battery-powered machine, and has a "Wrooom!" roaring electric motor that catches everyone's attention. It's like the helicopters you see in movies. Leo and Marta, too, are intrigued by the new, very mysterious child with the hat and his incredible pastime. Holding their favourite toys - the box of wonders and the marble bag - they approach him step by step.

"W-what's your name?" - Leo asks, his voice breaking with emotion. Even though he acts tough, he's really shy and always worried about people making fun of him.

"I'm Manuel, I just moved here! I don't know anyone yet, you know? Would you like to be my friend?" - asks the newcomer, smiling at him and offering his right hand.

Leo blushes. He didn't expect such a direct question!

"Of course!" - he replies without hesitation, with a strong handshake.

"I play alone almost all the time, too, because my dad is very busy with work and he doesn't have much time to play with me ..." - Leo continues, looking down. He doesn't want to admit it, but sharing his marbles with someone else is something... he doesn't mind at all! He's been bored for the past few weeks, but he doesn't have the courage to ask the other kids to play with him. It's amazing to have Manuel here. Finally, he'll be able to enjoy the last weeks of summer with a new, very nice friend... with a bit of a funny hat!

In the end, Leo and Manuel become in-se-pa-ra-ble! They meet at eight o'clock sharp at the beach kiosk - a small, multicoloured gazebo where Clara, the very kind owner, sells all kinds of sweets, ice cream of all shapes, pizza with stringy mozzarella, and lots of sugary drinks to cool off in the hottest hours - and have a mad dash. Who's gonna be the fastest and dive first?

Marta observes them from afar while wearing the jewels her Spanish "Abuela" gave her, or preparing tea for her favourite dolls. In her heart, she, too, would like to find a friend with a capital "F", someone to play with on the sand or in the waves. However, like Leo, she's afraid of looking like a loser if she takes the first step. She doesn't know exactly what the word loser means, but a few months earlier, she heard her big sister Cinzia shout it at a classmate. The unfortunate girl burst into tears in front of the whole school and the chemistry teacher wrote a note in Cinzia's diary, which made their parents very angry. After that, Marta made a pact with herself: she won't become a loser, never, ever... whatever that means. And she'll never make fun of anyone! As the last week of vacation approaches - when the older kids do their homework (a little late) under Clara's gazebo and the adults keep saying "I'd rather not go back to work", or "I'd rather do nothing all day long" - Marta, Leo, and Manuel embark on a very curious adventure in the sand.

Here's what happened.

On that extraordinary, revolutionary and magical August morning, Leo arrives at the ice cream stand on time.

"Phew, Manuel is always late!" - he grumbles, waving at Mrs. Clara, who sells ice creams to all the children on the beach.

"Don't lose heart!" - she says, handing him a glass of fresh water. «By the way, are you and Manuel going to participate in the super mega awesome tournament this afternoon? Are you ready? Are you all charged up?" - she asks, rubbing her hands in excitement.

Leo frowns, staring at her with a doubtful look on his face.

"Leo, I don't believe it! Don't you know about the marble tournament at the nearby lido? You are the King of Marbles!" - Clara continues, blinking with an incredulous expression on her face.

«No, I don't know anything about it ...» - Leo grumbles. He grabs Clara's promotional flyer and seals his lips in stubborn and regretful silence. He feels sad because neither his father, Manuel, nor anyone else at the beach knows about it. He would have loved to show off his marble skills! His dad might even pat him on the back and be proud of him.

"But it's too late now!" - he says to Manuel, who has joined him on the beach and asked him why he has a long face.

"Too late? Well, my friend, it's never too late!" - he shouts, standing up and pulling Leo by one foot, lifting sand on both sides. "We just need a… plan! Yes, a plan like Agent 007 or Iron-Man. Like Iron-Man! By the way, do you prefer Iron-

Man or Thor? Listen, forget it, every second is precious! The leaflet says that ... " - he says, observing him from every angle like a little chemist studying molecules under his microscope.

"Yes, he says we have to build the best marble track in... HISTORY! Whoever's faster, better, and more spectacular wins..."

I'm stopping you right now. Digging a long and deep track takes days... And we've only got four hours until the tournament starts. We're out, Manuel! Come on, let's go for a swim, maybe the sadness will pass... " - Leo grumbles.

"Well, don't forget we've got an ace up our sleeves..."

"W-what? What would it be? You didn't tell me your dad builds buildings and skyscrapers ... " - Leo exclaims, raising an eyebrow.

"No, not my dad, but ... MY TRUCK!" - Manuel shouts, unable to contain his excitement. Thanks to his good humour, he managed to revive his little friend's spirit! The radio-controlled truck would help them dig the best track on the beach in record time, without needing rakes, buckets, or a lot of effort. It's not all lost, Manuel might be right!

The two kids get to work right away. They draw the track with a thin branch; a very long track full of bends and bumps, ups and downs, and breathtaking turns. Leo will be the only one who can splash his marbles at the speed of light, astonishing the judges.

The hours pass quickly as the two little architects control the joystick of the remote-controlled truck to create a spectacular track. Occasionally, they dive into the hole to compact the sand, wet it with seawater, and decorate it with molds of toy cars, fish, and lifebuoys. Curious kids, cheering for Leo and Manuel's incredible feat, run to the beach to collect shells to place along the track. In short, their marble track path deserves the front page. Indeed, a whole magazine!

It's half an hour before the tournament, and everything's ready. Clara gives Manuel and Leo some pretty multicoloured flags to adorn the finish line, while Manuel's mom writes their names on the bright red billboard.

She smiles satisfied and says, "So everyone will know you're great."

"Okay, Manuel! Now let's go get the marbles under my umbrella and run to the track. It's only ten minutes away, we can do it! " says Leo, who can't wait to share the news with his dad. But when he approaches the blue and white striped umbrella - the closest to the coast - his mind goes back to an unexpected event: while transporting his bag that morning, the marble net bag tore, spilling the transparent marbles on the bottom of the backpack, on the sand, and between the pages of his mom's favourite newspaper.

"No, no, no! I can't believe it! We'll never make it!" Leo exclaims, as two warm tears stream down his cheeks. Manual doesn't know what to do to help his friend; it seems impossible to get to the site of the tournament in under ten minutes. Also, Leo might get disqualified if he doesn't have a bag of marbles.

"Do you have any idea?" - Manuel asks, looking for a bucket to carry the small transparent spheres. Their toys are still piled along the track, and Leo's backpack is filled with clothes, sunscreen, bottles of water, crosswords, and spare sandals. Oh yeah, there are some ham and cheese sandwiches too - to be precise.

Suddenly, a mysterious voice whispers: "I-I might have an idea ..."

The voice of a little girl.

Leo and Manuel turn abruptly, their eyes full of hope. With a toothy smile, Marta approaches the two friends.

"You need a box for your marbles, right? Well, here it is! " - she exclaims, handing her precious wooden box into Leo's hands. Manuel opens his mouth in disbelief, with the face of a... boiled fish!

"Marta, are you really giving us your magic box? Are you sure? Sure, sure, sure?" Manuel asks, staring at Leo and Marta as if he'd just met his favourite actor.

"Before I change your mind ..." she smiles, nodding. Without thinking twice, she bends down over the sand and starts picking up Leo's marbles.

One, two, three, ten, twenty, thirty, thirty-one, thirty-two, thirty-three and ...

they are all there!

The three friends can't wait to get started: they start running towards the lido to participate in the competition and make it to the wonderful track dug by Leo and Manuel two minutes before the start of the tournament. Leo grabs his beloved spheres from the wooden box that Marta lent him, he gets in position and - under the watchful eye of the judges - throws the first ball with pinpoint accuracy. Just like professional golf, baseball, or pool players! One after the other, the magical, colourful spheres of the talented Leo appear on the sandy track the two friends dug in the afternoon with the help of Manuel's remote-controlled truck. His skill leaves everyone - including the examiners - speechless. Dad, mom, and Clara watch Leo's performance, too, clapping their hands excitedly. Curve after curve, finger snap after finger snap, all the adults and children of the lido gather around Leo, cheering and admiring him.

Finally, when all the marbles reach the finish flag, Leo thanks the judges and runs towards his family and his new friends for a group hug. Observing him tenderly, dad dishevels his dark hair. "How come I've never noticed your skills all these years?" - he asks, then adds: *"you are amazing, Leo!"*.

Manuel and Marta approach the new marble champion.

"And now let's see who wins!" - they exclaim in chorus, observing the judges with a threatening expression, as if to say "and choose well, you two!"

"I don't care! Why don't we all celebrate together at Clara's kiosk?" Leo exclaims, holding his mother's hand.

"What do you mean? Don't you want to know who the winner is? I thought you wanted the King of Marbles medal

... and I really think it will be yours! " she says.

"No, because I've already won! Dad said I'm good, Clara gave me some colourful flags, you wrote a beautiful poster, and I also met Leo and Marta, two friends I'll always hold dear to my heart. Without you, this wouldn't have been possible! Thank you, thank you all!"

And you know what, my little reader?

Leo was totally right.

Many years ago, someone shared a quote that fits perfectly. I'm talking about a Greek poet with a pretty complicated name, Alekos Panagoulis. This is what he said:
Even when you know you're going to lose, <u>you still have to fight</u>. Because what matters isn't winning or losing: it's fighting."

The author says...

My friend, I bet you've heard the phrase "it's not about winning, it's about participating" a thousand times.

I guessed it right, didn't I?

The quote by Pierre De Coubertin was pronounced during the Olympic Games: every four years, the best athletes come together to compete in a great stadium with respect, cooperation, integrity, and willingness, to put themselves to the test. There's no doubt that Leo, the protagonist of the story, deserves an Olympic medal in "marbles racing"! Because whether it's a sports competition, a school project, a competition between friends, or a game of cards, the goal isn't to win, but to face the challenge as best as you can. That's the only way we'll be valid opponents, like Japanese samurai who respect their enemies. In short, everyday life is an excuse to have fun, integrate, meet new friends, and... make the world a better place, step by step!

In today's world, we often get messages that are very negative: it's like feeling bad because we didn't finish first, because we're not the best in class, or in sports, or on social media. Here's a question for you: have you ever entered a Likes and Followers challenge on Instagram, Facebook, and Tik Tok? How did you feel? Have you ever thought you're not good-looking, smart, charismatic, funny, and talented enough to become like your favourite YouTubers and Influencers? If so, what have you done to get over the sadness? Have you ever tried to improve yourself and achieve your goals no matter the cost, or have you preferred to focus on other things like studying, sports, music, theatre, or learning a foreign language?

Regardless of your past experiences, I have good news for you: it's all about changing your <u>attitude</u>.

It's called mindset!

Don't let yourself down and don't compare yourself to others who seem better. After all, you never know what fears, weaknesses, worries, and accidents your idols, your super smart classmates, or the VIPs who appear on your phone may have. Leo teaches us rule number 1 of true champions:

getting on the podium isn't important if you haven't met special people who've made you a better person during the competition.

Even if Leo had won the "King of Marbles" medal without his mom, Clara, Manuel, and Marta helping him, he wouldn't have been happy. The reason? He wouldn't have shown his dad he was a real talent, he wouldn't have made so many special friends along the way, and he wouldn't have had fun. The real victory lies in the generosity of the people who helped him realize his dreams, one piece at a time.

So, my little reader, dream big! When you're feeling down, focus on your priorities and the things that really matter. Make sure you work hard and consistently, have fun, and share your wins and losses with your parents and the people you love the most. The reason? Pierre De Coubertin reminds us once again that "the essential thing is not to win, but to fight well."

And to give our best - I would add.

PLANETS, MUSICAL NOTES AND BASKETBALL GAMES

A story of hope, change and dreams at high altitude

September 18th

Dear diary, I'm always asked: "What will you do when you grow up?" I don't understand why I should tell grown-ups what job I want to do in the future when first I have to finish elementary school, middle school, and high school - quite a challenge considering how much time my sister Alice spends on schoolbooks. They all look at me with curious expressions and expect me to say things like "the astronaut", "the policeman" or "the veterinary surgeon". In short, adults are really annoying: they don't seem to know what they're doing in life, but they poke their noses into everything kids do.

Wow!

To be honest, I recently found out what I want to do when I grow up. Since I don't want to spill it at the four winds because then the adults start asking me two thousand questions, I've decided to write my special secrets in the diary Aunt Alessia gave me on my birthday. And I always laugh, because my aunt's house really smells of flowers and she works hard so that anyone who sets foot in it always says:

"what a coincidence! I'm very envious of your green thumb!" and similar phrases. So - I was saying - I don't want to reveal my secrets.

But, well, when I grow up I want to be ... a basketball player! Yes, because I really don't like any other sports. Football is boring - and it is pretty predictable, everyone plays it. Ping-pong gives me a headache, while boxing is too dangerous and my mum told me there's no way I could enrol... Basketball, on the other hand, is something entirely different: the players are very tall and muscular, they play in America and are applauded by millions of people. My favourite team is little known, but I don't care: when I grow up I want to play as a forward for the Minnesota Timberwolves - a truly unpronounceable name that I have only heard once and can hardly remember well. I love basketball: I have posters in my bedroom, magazines with the latest NBA games (which is like the major league in football) and a truckload of cards and stickers dad bought me in a small second-hand shop down town. Therefore, if an adult asks me why I want to be a Minnesota Timberwolves player, I'll answer: «First of all, who gave you permission to read my diary, you rascal?

And then, I don't feel like wearing boring t-shirts all my life. I'm going to have the number 13 of the Minnesota Timberwolves and eat all the American burgers. Are you jealous? I know!"

Anyway, I hope no one reads this diary because my classmates say that writing in a diary is a bit of a "girly" thing. I think they're just jealous!

Michele

Dear diary, you have no idea what happened today. There are two new kids in class: Alma has long, curly, red hair with freckles on her cheeks, while Giovanni is one of those super-intelligent kids with glasses you see on TV. In gym class, the teacher put us on the same team to pull the rope and run the relay, and I really enjoyed it. Do you know why? Because Alma, at one point, said:

"I think adults are boring, they always ask the same questions. Like... what do you want to do when you grow up?" So I said I couldn't stand them - especially those second degree aunts with moustaches and flowered dresses you only see once a year during Christmas. We burst into laughter and, without even realizing it, we became friends. Because when three kids immediately understand each other, there is no need to use words: they become allies, just like in video games!

Before the end of the lesson, Giovanni lowered his voice, observed us with an intelligent look and said: "you know, when I grow up I want to learn all about the planets, go to the moon, and live on a spaceship that I'll build myself, with my dad's help!"

Alma and I stared at him with wide eyes and open mouths.
It's an incredible dream - I thought. I was a little embarrassed by my dream of becoming a Minnesota Timberwolves forward - which surely Giovanni didn't know - so I told them a lie, that I wanted to be a super-cool scientist in a very mysterious research lab in America. In America, yes, because I still want to eat all the burgers you see in the movies, even if I don't become a very tall basketball player. Finally, Alma turned purple in the face and quietly revealed her great dream: she wants to become someone who plays the ~~clarenette~~, the ~~clorinet~~ ... ah, what a complicated word!
The clarinet! Alma wants to play the clarinet - which is a flute, she explained - in a very important band whose name I forgot and where her mother also played the piano.

Dear Diary, dad shared some incredible news. He's finally found me an indoor basketball court where I can train even when it's cold and rainy. It's near grandma's house and the school where Alice takes Latin lessons. I'm ready to start my professional sports career! I'm looking forward to learning feints and slam dunks to confuse my opponents, especially the Cleveland Cavaliers, who I really dislike. As a kid, my dad was a defender in a football team, so he knew how hard it was to become a star.

Then, to cope with not making it to the national team, he took a karate class and learned self-defense. Bored with following the rules of a pseudo-Japanese master, he then signed up for a gym membership and bought all the gym equipment needed to build muscle like a Marvel superhero. It's safe to say he went there two, three times at most... without success!

Now that he's got a belly, he's stopped all his sports adventures, but he was really happy when I whispered in his ear that I wanted to play for the Minnesota Timberwolves. He got up from his chair in a hurry and said to me: "then you need a pitch to train on. How are you going to become a champion without a ball and a basket? I'll take care of it, give me a couple of days!"

On Monday, after work, he returned home with a mysterious plastic bag. Inside were the most beautiful red and white shoes I've ever seen, plus an NBA wristband and a black and white basketball that I loved - because it wasn't the classic you see in movies. It's heavy and doesn't quite fit in my hands, but I'll quickly get used to it. Then it was training time. The first session with the coach and the team is on October 5th, and I'm a little nervous.

What if I'm not as good as I think? Well, I guess in the end I can be an American scientist, as I told Giovanni, or follow in the footsteps of my dad, who works in a toy factory and makes lots of kids happy. I keep telling myself that I have so many possibilities to become an extraordinary adult. An adult full of passions and talents!

Dear Diary, I haven't written in a while, so I hope you're not mad at me. My schedule has been crazy: I train twice a week, on Tuesdays and Fridays. When I don't have math or history tests, I take my bike and get there even on Thursday afternoons. In the meantime, Alma, Giovanni and I have become good friends, even though they keep asking me why I became so mysterious two or three times a week. I told them I take private English lessons in a very exclusive school: "it is important for my future as an American scientist" - I said, trying to give my lie a bit of credibility. Giovanni nodded with emotion in his eyes, while Alma looked at me with an inquisitive look. She looked like one of those TV policewomen who find the culprits at first sight!

How stressful, my God!

I ignored that and tried to change the subject. And you know something strange, Dear Diary? I'm a little sad, because my friends would never understand my passion for basketball: they are smart, good, nice and capable of extraordinary things! Alma with her strange flute, while Giovanni with his astronomy books and a weird obsession for a hundred-year-old guy named ... Galileo Galilei, or something like that! I wonder: how is it possible to have almost the same name and surname? I am Michele, but not Michele Di Michele. It would sound terrible and everyone would make fun of me. Poor Galileo Galilei! Honestly, I think Giovanni is the only one who remembers him after all these years!

Emergency meeting, emergency meeting!

Dear Diary, I'm in a desperate situation. In fact, I'm in a lot of trouble. Even Napoleon Bonaparte wasn't so unlucky at Waterloo (I studied him in History class last week).

Things went more or less like this.
The coach gave me fantastic news: I will be one of the first-string players at the next game.

Yep, exactly!

I will have my own t-shirt, an identification number for the commentary and a lot of spectators watching me score the winning point two seconds before the end of the game. I can't wait to get out there and give it my all!

The problem?

Dad wants to invite my classmates to cheer for me.

"You know, Michele" - he told me - "it's important not to be alone during the first game of the season! We'll build a colourful billboard and give you all the energy you need to score the first points!"

Yes, I could have said no - that I prefer to focus on my own - and that the presence of my classmates would only made me nervous - but I was watching my favourite cartoon and ... I let my guard down! The coach told me "never let your guard down on the pitch", and I fell into my dad's trap without even noticing.

Three-pointer? Score!

When I went to the kitchen for breakfast this morning, I almost tripped over a packet of brochures and flyers my dad' office secretary had printed for all my classmates. Actually, for all the children of the world judging by their number!

"A-are you crazy?" - I yelled at him, because I couldn't believe my eyes. Surely, if just one flyer had accidentally fallen into Alma and Giovanni's hands, they would have discovered the lie, they would have figured out I'm not as smart as I want them to believe, and they would have laughed at me.

I can't let that happen!

«D-Dad, now that I think about it... I don't know if it's a good idea! I might make a fool of myself in front of everyone... I really don't want anyone to know about the next match!" - I told him, trying to crumple a handful of flyers. I had to "destroy evidence" like the bad guys in the crime movies mummy likes so much. But my dad isn't one to give up easily, and he tells me he's already invited Mattia and Genny, whose parents are old family friends. It was at that point that I went white as a sheet and invisible as a ghost, because Mattia is the most gossipy and chatty kid I have ever known!

Help, I'm desperate!

I grabbed a few more invitations and ran to my room.

Dear Diary, do you have a solution? Maybe you're smarter than me and can help me out of this mess. I can make up another lie and tell Giovanni and Alma I was invited at the last minute. "I don't like basketball, but I have a natural talent and I'm essential to winning this championship game"- I can say. Maybe I'll add: "After all, real scientists have to stay fit, they can't just eat American hamburgers for life!" Well, that sounds awesome!After all, real scientists also have to keep fit, it's not like they can only eat American hamburgers for life!" Well, it sounds like a great idea!

What do you think, Dear Diary? I knew that talking to you would help me find a brilliant solution! Now that I think of it, maybe I can still become a super smart chemist or biologist, right?

C'mon, c'mon, the Minnesota Timberwolves *are waiting for me!*

November, 2nd

65 - 77

We won

I scored thirteen points, including a three-pointer that left the coach speechless (and my dad, who was in the bleachers). I'd like to be happy and enjoy the pizza and fries that Mom promised me to order from the best pizzeria in town - Dear Diary, it's truly sensational! - but I had an argument with Giovanni and Alma. When I arrived in class and repeated the lie I'd made up with you, they looked at me with an angry expression. I shivered! That blabbermouth Matteo had already told everyone about my awesome sporting prowess, saying that I trained three times a week on a field near the school. Basically, my father hadn't been able to hold back and told his friends everything about my monthly training over the phone!

My special secret was now public knowledge.

Alma gave me a dirty look and asked: "Why did you lie to us?"

My cheeks flushed and tears filled my eyes. But I didn't want to cry, not before the most important game of the season.

"I-it's not a lie! I didn't really train... »- I answered shyly.

Giovanni took off his thick eyeglasses, put them on the desk, and looked into my eyes. "Micky, we're friends.". Friends don't lie for weeks. W-why did you do it?"

Oh yes, I wanted to sink into the school tiles and disappear.

I met Alma and Giovanni in the gym's locker room, where no one could hear us. And, with a slightly broken voice, I explained that I didn't want to sound like an unintelligent kid who has no interests or talent. Alma had her beautiful clarinet, while Giovanni had an innate talent for the stars and planets in the sky. And me? I just wanted to eat hamburgers and fries in America and be an NBA star. What a deal! Everyone can throw the ball into a basket with a little practice and some luck! And then, to be honest, I'm too short to be like Kobe Bryant.

They looked at me a little confused and then burst into laughter. Alma rolled on the ground, holding her belly as

Giovanni beat his fists on the wooden bench.

"W-what? You're laughing at me, I can't believe it!" - I screamed, my face swollen with anger. What a nerve! First they got mad because I told them a lie, and now they're acting so... so... ah, I don't even know how to describe them!

I yelled, "WE ARE NOT FRIENDS ... never again!", And I ran out of the gym to get some fresh air. My hands were shaking and I felt angry, very angry. I quickly rode my bike home, where my parents were waiting for me with a bright red jersey for the game. I slammed the door, locked myself in my bedroom and ... counted to ten! I stretched my leg muscles, hopped on the spot, and looked at the Minnesota Timberwolves poster I hung above the textbook shelf to keep my spirits up even when I can't understand maths.

And the game went well, very well.

However, I can't help but think it would have been much

better if Alma and Giovanni had been there.

Dear Diary, get ready because I'm going to tell you an incredible story today.

I'm at school at eight in the morning, not a second later or earlier. I lock my bike, put the keys in my pockets and when I turn around, Alma's honey-coloured gaze greets me. She has red cheeks from the cold, a hat with a pom-pom on, and her usual sly expression.

"W-what's up?" - I tell her, trying to sound like a real ... macho!
«Mh, nothing" - she mumbles. " I was just wondering where you learned to dribble between the legs. You know, right? The one that made you score the third point! That was really cool! " - she whispers, with a conspiratorial look.

No idea if it's emotion, surprise, or just that I'm truly happy with my move as a real NBA star, but I burst into a liberating laugh that also infects Alma.

"YOU CAME? Aaah, I knew you were coming!" - I tell her, throwing my arms around her. Suddenly, just as I let my guard down, a familiar hand slaps me on the shoulder. It's Giovanni!

"Not to mention the three-pointer! I swear to you, the guy next to me widened his eyes and said, "That kid will go a long way, I know." Do you know what I told him? That he was right. Besides an American scientist, you'll be the best point guard in a few years!"

"So, you don't think basketball is a... stupid thing?" - I ask, looking down.

"Stupid ?! What are you talking about? It's so cool!" - says Alma. "I'd never seen a basketball game live before, and it was awesome... And then they serve mouth-watering popcorn in the sports hall!"

«I know, Alma, you ate mine too ...» - Giovanni mutters.

"So are we friends again?" You're not mad at me, are you? " - I ask.

"Friends like before", Giovanni exclaims. "But on one condition ..."

"No lies?" - I echo.

Obviously! But you have to promise us something else... If you become a world star, Alma and I will always have front-row seats. For free, of course! Don't be stingy! I can't wait to visit the States!" - and they burst into laughter.

"Promised, promised! But only if you, Alma, invite Giovanni and me to all your clarinet concerts! " - I say.

"And you, Giovanni, you should dedicate a star to us, perhaps an unknown planet!" Alma says, staring up at the sky with a dreamy expression. "The star of Almichael, of Michaelama ... Oh, I'm not good at inventing names!"

Dear diary, we were silent for a few minutes waiting for the bell to ring. All of us - I'm sure - thought about the future that awaited us. Alma would have jumped from one score to another with her long tapered fingers, playing sweet notes with the elegant clarinet. Giovanni would have dedicated his life to science, and I would have tried to win the title with the Minnesota Timberwolves against the Cleveland Cavaliers. And do you know why? Because we're a close-knit team, and if we dream together... we can make our dreams a reality!

My little friend, I want to tell you a secret.

Get a little closer, because it's really top secret.

Here's the Michele of the story - drum roll, ta-ta-ta-ta-ta - it's me, the pen that's writing the little book of stories you have in your hands!

You d*on't you believe me?*

You know, when I was eight, I was a huge fan of basketball. Not only did I watch every game on TV, sipping Coke, hot tea, and refreshing slushes, but I had every single issue of the official NBA magazine that I bought with my first pocket money. Obviously, all the articles were in English, and I knew only a few words back then - like *hello, how are you ?, my name is… and the cat is on the table!*

The Minnesota Timberwolves was precisely were favourite

team, and they had this super-fascinating logo I copied with some tissue paper and drew on the first page of my math notebook!

I was a very creative child.

I can almost imagine what's going through your head at this point: "listen, Serena R. Mancini, how come you became a writer and not an NBA star who lives in America and drives a bright red Ferrari?"

Okay, okay, I owe you an explanation!

Honestly, my little friend, over time my desires have changed, my needs have changed, and my childhood dreams have been replaced by other ones. After playing basketball for ten long years, I chose to become a journalist, a writer, a publisher, and to do everything that's related to words!

In short, I found my way in life!

Have you ever watched Disney's animated classic "Alice in Wonderland"? If so, I'm sure you'll remember the cute

Cheshire Cat that pops up in the protagonist's life with its funny oddness. Well, I've always liked something the pink-and-purple cat says at one point: "if you don't know where you're going, then it doesn't matter which way you go."

Go, that's the most important thing - I would add.

Maybe you think you don't have any talents nor dreams. You still don't know whether you should be a great dentist, a ballet teacher, a firefighter, or an internationally renowned musician.

Well, you know what?

It doesn't matter!

And you know why? Because it's hard to figure out the calling, talent and hobby that really makes you happy. It's a patience exercise that sometimes can last a lifetime. The world is full of people who choose to change jobs and habits - from bank clerk to globetrotter, from philosophy teacher to tango dancer - because they realise they are different. The past doesn't excite us anymore. We don't really enjoy old toys, and we think they're childish. Having started high school and university, we're spending less and less time with our friends from elementary school. In addition, our bodies change, we get taller, stronger, and our voices get more mature. We grow, always. We never stop growing. Similarly, at the age of eighteen I realized I didn't want to become the leader of my favourite team, that America didn't fascinate me like it used to, and that I wanted to write stories for a living. So here I am, pen in hand and tons of white paper on my desk. I don't live in the USA, I don't play basketball, and I don't watch NBA games with my family anymore. Now I live all alone in a small studio, I often change country, I am a big tennis fan and I no longer drink Coke, but delicious cups of steaming coffee instead.

I don't even see Alma and Carlo - who are Giulia and Lorenzo in real life - as much as I used to. We call each other once or twice a year to talk about our adventures around the world. Giulia plays the clarinet in Russia, while Lorenzo opened a pastry shop in Rome and prepares lots of colourful mouth-watering sweets - those covered in rainbow sprinkles. One thing is certain, though: even if time has divided our paths, we are still the three kids full of dreams who shared unforgettable moments among planets, musical notes, and basketball games.

I SAY NO TO BULLYING

Unity is strength against bullying!

I'm Barbara, I've got long hair below the shoulders and a slightly large, humped nose. I don't like the shape of my nose at all, it reminds me of the Hunchback of Notre-Dame, a cartoon that always scared me when I was a kid. Also, I'm an only child. My mum and my dad are fan-ta-stic and they always tell me: «we are a team, Bri!». I really like the idea of being part of a group. It makes me feel special and important to the people I love.

Suddenly, a noise catches my attention. I look up from the paper I'm holding in my hands. It's a notebook page where I wrote the speech I'll give tomorrow morning in front of the new students at the primary school where I'll work. Finally, after months - no, years - of mad studying, working, and substitutions around my country, I got my first professorship.

I'm a teacher!

I've fulfilled my lifelong dream!

When I got the news three weeks ago, I immediately started writing my presentation piece. I guess the new students are nervous, shy and a little scared. So one evening, while chatting with my better half on the couch, I thought I'd tell them a little about myself and my past. Like many, I was an awkward and (very) clumsy child. Like many, I've experienced the "nervous stomach" before a test or an oral exam. Like many, I've fought hard to feel accepted and respected by my little classmates - often with poor results.

So here I am, in the small room I use as a library-study, with the speech in my hands and Briciola's eyes watching me curiously. My inseparable four-legged friend wags its tail in delight, snuggles up on the polka dot pillow I bought over the weekend, and starts nibbling on a rubber bone. While it may not be an attentive and responsible student, my little dog is still the only pseudo-child I can practice tomorrow's presentation with.

Ah - certainly, it's never experienced the number 1 enemy of all kids: bullying.

We hear about it a lot in newspapers, TV shows, conferences, and school books, but not everyone knows what bullying means.

Bullying is:

✓   When kids get teased and bullied by their classmates.

✓   When they're left out of games, insulted, and don't get much respect. Some examples? The other kids steal their snacks, ruin their school supplies, take their money by force, or scribble on their books and notebooks.

✓   When a group of kids target the same schoolmates all the time. Many times, other kids want to stand up for them, but they're scared of becoming victims of the bullies themselves.

✓   When the kids being teased can't stand up for themselves.

In short, bullying happens whenever a child is threatened, punched or pinched repeatedly over time.

Bullying is whenever other kids ruin personal items like pencils, pencil cases, and diaries - or offend or exclude the victim.

Bullying is whenever bullies focus on a classmate's physical or behavioural flaws, tease him/her with extreme nastiness and insult him/her heavily.

As I write my speech, Briciola watches me with curious eyes. Can it sense my... agitation? Yes, because talking about bullying means facing our weaknesses and vulnerabilities. It means facing fears and challenges that seem bigger than us. When I was a kid, the world was very different from the one the students I'll meet in the morning live in. Anyhow, bullies already existed - in fact, they've always existed - and many adults have encountered rude or aggressive people at some point in their lives.

But let's go in order. When I, Barbara, wore the dark blue apron to face my first day of school with my heart in my mouth, things didn't go too bad. Mrs. Marisa observed the class with the sweetest and kindest eyes I'd ever seen - just like my grandmother - and spoke to us in a calm and angelic voice. Besides telling us about the wonderful adventures we'd have had together, she promised us theatre, music, and foreign language classes. Each of us would have studied basic subjects and engaged in some afternoon activities. Our meals from the canteen would have been prepared by the plump hands of Mrs. Anna, a retired cook who worked on cruise ships and toured exotic countries.

I was so happy!

But my happiness was destined to disappear as fast as a

Formula 1 car...

«*VROOOM!*»

When the bell rang for break, I was approached by a classmate I hadn't seen before. His name? Giacomo. He was tall and tough like a mountain, and he sat right behind me. So lucky, huh! He started reading other classmates' diaries and making jokes to pass the time. I immediately realised he was looking for an excuse to make trouble and act like a "I-know-it-all" ...

As he approached me, I looked down at the notebook and ate an apple nervously in small bites.

"What a boring diary, it's all green!" - he said, slamming his fist on my desk.

I kept my head down. I thought if I ignored him, he'd get bored and leave me alone. Well, I was wrong! My silence got him even more angry, so he yelled: "What are you doing?" Don't you speak English? What's your name?"

Sure, it was a simple question. I could have answered him "Barbara!" calmly, asking him to leave me alone so I could finish my snack. But I couldn't speak. I felt my cheeks burning with anger and shame, and the apple slipped from my hands in fear. When the fruit fell, the boy laughed mockingly.

"Oh, so you're a sucker who misses mommy ... Can't you even eat an apple without mommy?" - he began to shout, grabbing the class's attention." As I clenched my hand into a fist, my slightly sticky fingers trembled with frustration. Seeing me like that, he put his hands to his mouth as if he had a megaphone and yelled in my ear: "BOOOOH, loser!". Eventually, he run to the boys' bathroom before Mrs. Marisa could notice.

Thinking about it now, after years of experience in contact with children of all ages, I still wonder why that sound scared me so much. I remember the shivers on my skin, and a sense of helplessness and sadness growing inside me like wildfire. *I didn't answer anything, but I wanted to say many things.*

I didn't tell anyone, not even my teacher, my parents, or my classmates - the ones who liked me and wanted to hear my jokes. In any case, Giacomo's teasing got more aggressive and exhausting as time went on. My only respite was during the theatre class I began to attend (almost) every afternoon.

The school was staging "Pinocchio" and auditions were open for the Fox role.

"You're perfect!" - Mrs. Vittoria told me, putting the freshly printed script in my hands. My lines were underlined with a cute pink highlighter. Giacomo, on the other hand, was the goalkeeper of the soccer team and kept showing off his skills, always looking for an excuse to target me.

"Barbara should do some sport to get back in shape ... not theatre! She'll be like a ball in a few years" - he shouted, making his teammates laugh.

No surprise: bullies attack kids who are fragile, shy, or different. It's inevitable, it's their "job". They wouldn't be real bullies otherwise. However, experience taught me the first rule to beating even the most stubborn and annoying bullies in town: don't be swayed by their jokes. Bullies are dangerous when they make us believe we are ugly, fat, unpleasant, lonely, stupid, poor, or nerdy just like they think. As for me, Giacomo had no chance of lowering my self-esteem or spirits. Partly because I could always count on the support of my mom and dad, and partly because my passion for theatre grew ... and I wouldn't have traded it for a ping-pong or volleyball course! It wasn't long before I became best friends with the kids in the show, and even my classmates realised Giacomo's jokes were boring.

After yet another attack from the bully, my classmate Veronica patted me on the shoulder and said, "She's not so fat and dumb as you think."

"Only because you too are fat and stupid..." Giacomo replied, briskly walking away.

The second rule of defeating a bully is finding allies, supporters, and true friends who are willing to help us. It may seem commonplace, but it's not. As soon as I realised I was surrounded by great people in school and after-school theatre class, I felt stronger, better, and smarter. My parents were right, "unity is strength". I gradually started to get a lot of support from the silent spectators who respected Giacomo because they were scared of being teased or beaten.

"Hey, Giacomo... are you sure you're as good a goalkeeper as you say you are?"

"You're always here teasing Barbara and you never train..." - said Lapo, my amazing (and beautiful) stage partner who played the Cat in "Pinocchio".

"Giacomo, aren't you afraid of Barbara because she's the best actress on the show? You still have time if you wanna ask for an autograph..." - continued Luca, the Jiminy Cricket.

I found my team. I wasn't alone anymore.

As the months passed, I adopted one last, very important strategy. The third rule for beating a bully is self-irony.

What's this about?

Well, it's really simple!

I smiled before Giacomo could shout something like "Barbara has a witch's nose" or "Barbara is as fat as a whale" to my group of friends in the break. I waited for him outside the classroom and self-mocked before he could open his mouth.

"Did you see my nose today?" - I said.

"Hey, do you know that yesterday I ate a delicious pizza with buffalo mozzarella just to gain weight?" - I replied. At least you've got a valid reason to make fun of me ... »- I continued.

In short, thanks to the awesome people I met at school, I started using the same weapons as the bully to ...defend myself!

If I was teased for how I looked in a picture, I shrugged and said "It must have been the photographer's fault!". If I failed a math test and got a bad grade, I always asked the teacher if I could go to the blackboard to understand the exercise with her and the class. Giacomo's audience decreased day by day, question by question... just like his cruel jokes! The bully of the class started to deflate visibly, he avoided me and headed to the gym... with his tail between his legs!

Having the help of my friends saved me and made me a much stronger, more self-confident girl (first) and a woman (later).

When I look up from the page of my lined notebook, the sun is long gone. Briciola snoozes with its eyes closed, dreaming of who knows which sandy beach to run free on with its tongue hanging out. A little sleepy, I read the speech again, put the pencil on the desk, and recite the last sentence out loud:

"I told you my story so I could say the words I couldn't say on my first day of school many years ago. Now I hope you, too, can find your own words to say no to bullying this school year. Together!"

I like it.

After all, we can all become superheroes. We should never turn away from injustice, but stick together to fight it.

 **Bullying**. Have you ever been teased, bullied, or abused at school or in the locker room? Alternatively, have you ever behaved badly due to anger, fear, or agitation? Did you feel sorry for that? Did you apologise?

I want to use this short editorial space to give you some practical tips for warding off bullies. Because let's face it: too often, adults don't understand your suffering. That's normal! It's not easy to "go back to being a child" and put yourself in the shoes of a smart and intelligent kid like you.

But let's get straight to the point!

Here's what you can do if someone's misbehaving with you:

✓   The first thing you should do is tell your parents and teachers what happens in their absence. Grown-ups have a thousand thoughts on their minds and don't always see your behavioural signals. Therefore, I recommend you get over your embarrassment, approach them in a moment of calm, and tell them what happened that made you feel bad. Bullies who think they can get away with it could end up getting even bossier and more dangerous in the long run!

✓   Never think it's your fault. You're not responsible for a bully's bad behaviour. There's no reason to be ashamed of your uniqueness, whether it's your skin colour, your musical tastes, your body, or your grades. Nobody has the right to make fun of you and make you feel wrong. Never forget that diversity is an advantage and a precious resource!

✓   Make sure you're not alone when you might get bullied. As Barbara, the teacher in the story, said, **unity is strength!**

✓   Stay calm, don't be scared or angry, and look the bully in the eye... with serenity! You get targeted by bossy kids because they know you'll react badly. Bullies will quickly forget about you if you anticipate their moves or prove you're superior! What can you do when you notice someone bullying your classmate?

✓ Make sure you don't get involved in the bully's "show" and don't participate in pranks and abuse.

✓ Praising the victim's intelligence, kindness, or sympathy is a good way to show your disagreement with the bully's behaviour. You can convince undecided "bystanders" the bully's behaviour is wrong if you focus on another child's talents and strengths.

✓ Talk to the bully's victims and tell them to talk to a teacher or an adult.

If you're friends with the bully, tell him/her how and why he/she crossed the line.

Cyberbullying. My dear reader, have you ever come across a cyber super bully? Online, the bad guys are both on social networks - such as Instagram, Tik Tok and Facebook - and entertainment   sites (*YouTube, Reddit,   Twitch,* etc.). Here's how to virtually "knock them out" if they make useless, insulting comments about you.

Some examples?

Intrigued by the word cyberbullying, I took a 2.0 trip to YouTube and scrolled through the feedback left under the videos of a well-known professional YouTuber.

I *was* shocked*!*

Without words!

Bewildered!

There are some profiles - almost all of them without

photos or recognisable names - that write insults to both the channel owner and the users who just want to distract themselves and have fun.

Some examples?

"You suck and you don't make people laugh", or "You're fat, aren't you ashamed?", Or "you're gay, go hide"

You, a friend, or someone you know may have received such messages. To increase hatred and teasing, they invade WhatsApp chats and try to "steal" photos posted on social media.

Here's a super secret: **cyberbullying is a crime, so don't call it a joke.** I did some research online and found that 4 out of 10 kids are (or have been in the past) victims of digital bullying, according to the data shared by the CORECOM Communications System Control Committee. Some are the target of false gossip, some are the protagonists of private videos that circulate online with false descriptions, some get put in a bad light with their parents and teachers, etc.

Some 2.0 bullies open fake profiles on social networks and begin to "blackmail" the victim.

Now, keep two very important things in mind:

A)   Even if you share them publicly on Facebook or WhatsApp, no one can use your photos without your permission:

B)   Most of the time, web bullies are backed by other users who want to make fun of you.

Like traditional bullying, the advice I want to give you is to never be alone. Get help from your parents, teachers, and classmates - even better if they're older than you. And remember: it's never the victims' fault.

CONCLUSIONS

Five stories, five little life lessons.

Curiosity is a very important thing because it opens our eyes to all the nuances of this world. Start asking yourself the "whys" of the things around you!

Nature is full of surprises. Observing animals, plants, and Earth's manifestations can help us solve problems, invent things, and take care of the planet.

Cooperation is more important than winning. If we don't have friends, parents, and teachers who believe in us, what's the point of getting on the podium?

Dreams fuel our lives. Dreaming big means putting ourselves out there, accepting defeat, and changing year after year, knowing that we're talented and wonderful. Do you already know what your big desire is? What do you want to fulfil and turn into reality?

Bullying is the number one enemy of every child, but it can also be a chance to play as a team against aggressive and / or negative kids who are angry with us. Rather than being passive spectators, we should help others and ourselves.

My dear, little reader, I hope these short stories intrigued you, amused you, or - more simply - relaxed you before bedtime. As I wrote the first pages of the book you're holding, I asked myself: "What are the super-secret messages I wanted to know as a kid?"

I compiled lots of ideas and turned them into the little book that's just kept you company for a few hours.

Don't be afraid to talk to your parents if you're having any doubts. They'll be happy to answer your questions. If, however, you want to write down your thoughts and emotions in black and white, then take a new notebook, sharpen your pencil, and start writing a diary about your thoughts and emotions. No, this isn't a *girly thing*. Actually, it's for real literary geniuses! Every great writer has kept a diary to collect ideas and write drafts of chapters and scenes.

You'll feel liberated, happy, and satisfied after telling a white sheet about yourself.

Give it a try (and let me know what you think).

Finally, I turn to you, parents, teachers, and adults. It's true, the challenges our little explorers are facing give us a hard time. Most of the time, we feel helpless, passive, and light years away from the macrocosm of childish values we have long forgotten. However, if we roll up our sleeves and clear our minds of a few too many prejudices, we can rediscover the beauty, ingenuity, curiosity, spontaneity, and energy of child development. I'm talking about that time in life when the world is mysterious, school days seem endless, and parental support is everything. Here's my small piece of advice with you: **don't trivialise**.

Although the problems of a child or a student may seem negligible and insignificant when compared to bills, business meetings, and delicate family matters, children are not that different from us. They, too, navigate on a life raft in the wonderful, and sometimes frightening, ocean called life.

In the words of Gianni Rodari: "Is a bbook with two B's just heavier than the others, a wrong book, or a very special one?"

I'm going with the first hypothesis. If my collection of short stories was useful and kept you company from start to finish, please leave your personal, free and above all honest review to help me share it with as many young readers as possible..

A hug,

Serena R. Mancini

Printed in Great Britain
by Amazon

12292220R10071